Knock, knock!

Who's there?

_____
(your name)

_____ who?
(your name)

_____, Big Nate's #1 friend!
(your name)

Lincoln Peirce

BiG NATE

DOODLEPALOOZA

RHYME DRAW LAUGH DOODLE RHYME DRAW LAUGH DOODLE RHYME DRAW LAUGH DOODLE

HARPER
An Imprint of HarperCollinsPublishers

ISBN 978-0-06-211114-2 (trade bdg.)
ISBN 978-0-06-229202-5 (international ed.)

Typography by Andrea Vandergrift
13 14 15 16 17   LP/RRDH   10 9 8 7 6 5 4 3 2 1

First Edition

For Big Nate Fans All Over the World
Especially if you love—

messy closets
lotsa comix
cool trivia
ridiculous nicknames
the Jefferson Cavaliers
(Okay, forget about that last one.)

NATE-TASTIC TRIVIA

See how well YOU know Nate's world.

1. Gordie, Ellen's boyfriend, can draw with both hands at the same time.
   ☐ TRUE   ☐ FALSE

2. One of Nate's favorite comics is "Femme Fatale."
   ☐ TRUE   ☐ FALSE

3. Artur makes double-chocolate cookies for Nate.
   ☐ TRUE   ☐ FALSE

4. Nate's neighbor, Mr. Eustis, once went to a polka festival.
   ☐ TRUE   ☐ FALSE

Mr. Eustis ←

5. Nate plays Captain Hook in P.S. 38's production of "Peter Pan."
   ☐ TRUE   ☐ FALSE

BLAST YOU, PETER PAN!

SWOOSH!

6. Nate's science teacher, Mr. Galvin, was once a Timber Scout.

□ TRUE   □ FALSE

7. The wall hangings Nate sells for his scout troop are called "Off the Wall Words."

□ TRUE   □ FALSE

8. Nate was grounded for shaving Spitsy.

□ TRUE   □ FALSE

9. Nate accidentally chopped the foot off a garden gnome.

□ TRUE   □ FALSE

10. Gina's in love with Artur.

□ TRUE   □ FALSE

MOVIE MADNESS

You're in the director's chair now! Fill in the speech bubbles and decide what happens.

THE END

DANCE DISASTERS

In Nate's opinion, these 4 are the worst dancers at P.S. 38. Fill out the grid so they all appear once in each row, column, and box.

S = **MR. STAPLES**

F = **FRANCIS**

K = **KIM CRESSLY**

Q = **SETH "Q-TIP" QUINCY**

CLOSET CRISIS!

Beware! Nate's closet is overflowing with stuff. Help Nate out and see if you can find all 25 things!

SOCCER CLEATS

THERMOS

NOTEBOOK

SWEATSHIRT

PLAYING CARDS

BUG HOUSE

FOOTBALL

MONOPOLY

RUBIX CUBE

HULA HOOP

RAINCOAT

COMIC BOOKS

BANANA PEEL

ACTION FIGURE

MICKEY MOUSE EARS

MOLDY TUNA SANDWICH

STINKY GYM SHORTS

YO-YO

REPORT CARD

BASEBALL CAP

MATH NOTES

UNDERWEAR

SLINKY

GUMMI BEARS

TIMBER SCOUT UNIFORM

```
E M N C N U F E P A C L L A B E S A B F R
M E O U U A A S R A I N C O A T R T O M S
Y I T L N O A U S C W U M P R I S O I O O
I O E R D E E O S E G M L O D M T C C U M
W R B E E Y U H L U R A H L O B K C O P O
E B O P R A T G T T Y S O N A E E O M O H
U U O O W F N U T I M I O L Y R R A T R C
O O K R E S O B N Y O P L M C S U X A O D
M E O T A D E G G A O R O L L C G A U M R
U M S C R Y C Y Y L S U E I E O I L E U N
S O H A T A K D Y T S A N H Y U F U E A E
C N A R R N D E U E T K N O T T N S O Y G
O R U D I O P K E S Y A Y D I U O E O C A
S Y S T H U L A H O O P E R W N I T L T I
O O S S S O R U B I X C U B E I T O O O T
D A M S T S K O O B C I M O C F C N C C N
D K S R A E B I M M U G A S O O A H I W C
H A L E E P A N A N A B C R E R B T B R T
I S T N W H O S O T N I A L W M C A P T S
D F N M S S T B E S D E S R B E H M T I B
O R S S I R B R O B S E K I S R G S A R I
```

my closet →

KSSSCH!!

WARM FUZZIES

Solve the maze to find out who's going to buy a Warm Fuzzy from Nate.

DANGER!
DOODLE ZONE

Leave those neat notes behind!

This is a place for doodles ONLY.

SERIOUSLY SMART

Francis is hooked on facts! Use his special code to uncover wacky animal trivia!

A	B	C	D	E	F	G	H	I	J	K	L	M
13	7	26	25	8	16	3	1	20	4	12	23	18

N	O	P	Q	R	S	T	U	V	W	X	Y	Z
21	11	2	15	14	24	6	10	19	22	17	9	5

$\overline{}$ 13

$\overline{}$ 25 $\overline{}$ 14 $\overline{}$ 13 $\overline{}$ 3 $\overline{}$ 11 $\overline{}$ 21 $\overline{}$ 16 $\overline{}$ 23 $\overline{}$ 9

$\overline{}$ 1 $\overline{}$ 13 $\overline{}$ 24 $\overline{}$ 13

$\overline{}$ 23 $\overline{}$ 20 $\overline{}$ 16 $\overline{}$ 8 $\overline{}$ 24 $\overline{}$ 2 $\overline{}$ 13 $\overline{}$ 21 $\overline{}$ 11 $\overline{}$ 16

$\overline{}$ 6 $\overline{}$ 22 $\overline{}$ 8 $\overline{}$ 21 $\overline{}$ 6 $\overline{}$ 9

$\overline{}$ 16 $\overline{}$ 11 $\overline{}$ 10 $\overline{}$ 14

$\overline{}$ 1 $\overline{}$ 11 $\overline{}$ 10 $\overline{}$ 14 $\overline{}$ 24 .

$\overline{26}\ \overline{14}\ \overline{20}\ \overline{26}\ \overline{12}\ \overline{8}\ \overline{6}\ \overline{24}\quad \overline{1}\ \overline{8}\ \overline{13}\ \overline{14}$

$\overline{6}\ \overline{1}\ \overline{14}\ \overline{11}\ \overline{10}\ \overline{3}\ \overline{1}\quad \overline{6}\ \overline{1}\ \overline{8}\ \overline{20}\ \overline{14}$

$\overline{12}\ \overline{21}\ \overline{8}\ \overline{8}\ \overline{24}.$

$\overline{6}\ \overline{1}\ \overline{8}\quad \overline{13}\ \overline{19}\ \overline{8}\ \overline{14}\ \overline{13}\ \overline{3}\ \overline{8}$

$\overline{1}\ \overline{8}\ \overline{21}\quad \overline{22}\ \overline{20}\ \overline{23}\ \overline{23}\quad \overline{23}\ \overline{13}\ \overline{9}$

$\overline{6}\ \overline{22}\ \overline{11}\quad \overline{1}\ \overline{10}\ \overline{21}\ \overline{25}\ \overline{14}\ \overline{8}\ \overline{25}$

$\overline{13}\ \overline{21}\ \overline{25}\quad \overline{6}\ \overline{22}\ \overline{8}\ \overline{21}\ \overline{6}\ \overline{9}$

$\overline{24}\ \overline{8}\ \overline{19}\ \overline{8}\ \overline{21}\quad \overline{8}\ \overline{3}\ \overline{3}\ \overline{24}$

$\overline{13}\quad \overline{9}\ \overline{8}\ \overline{13}\ \overline{14}.$

LIFE IS A DRAMA

What's happening? Fill in all the speech bubbles (and decode the captions) and become the scriptwriter.

A ⊕
B ⊕
C ⊕
D ⊕
E ⊕
F ⊕
G ⊕
H ⊕
I ⊕
J ⊕
K ⊕
L ⊕
M ⊕
N ⊕
O ⊕
P ⊕
Q ⊕
R ⊕
S ⊕
T ⊕
U ⊕
V ⊕
W ⊕
X ⊕
Y ⊕
Z ⊕

⊕⊕⊕⊕⊕ ⊕ ⊕⊕⊕⊕⊕⊕⊕⊕ ⊕⊕⊕'⊕ ⊕⊕⊕⊕!

⊕⊕⊕⊕⊕⊕ ⊕⊕⊕⊕⊕⊕⊕ ⊕⊕?

⊕⊕⊕⊕'⊕ ⊕⊕⊕ ⊕⊕⊕⊕ ⊕⊕⊕⊕⊕⊕?

SCRIBBLE CHALLENGE

1. MAKE A SCRIBBLE.

Don't take longer than 2 seconds.

MY BEST DRAWING PEN

Don't make it too complicated.

2. TURN YOUR SCRIBBLE INTO A DRAWING.

Don't erase!

Have fun!

For challenge, close your eyes to scribble.

Add a caption!

AMAZING ARTUR

Nate's competing with his rival, Artur, again! What does Nate have to say about it? You decide!

WHEN I GROW UP

Do you dream about who you'll be when you grow up? Nate wants to be a famous cartoonist. List your dream careers, then rank them from 1 (ho-hum) to 20 (yahoo!).

_____ Scout leader   _____
_____   _____
_____   _____
_____   _____
_____   _____ Professional
_____ Dog whisperer   skateboarder
_____
_____
                            GATHER 'ROUND!
_____ Park ranger
_____
_____
_____ Astronomer

MASCOT MADNESS

Nate's school, P.S. 38, has a pretty great mascot: the bobcat! But their rival, Jefferson Middle School, always brags that their cavalier is cooler. What do you think?

CIRCLE THE BEST MASCOT IN EACH ROW!

Tiger	Warrior	Diamondback
Cardinal	Cougar	Psycho Dog
Jazz	Bear	Viking
Mariner	Jet	Dolphin
Eagle	Kuddle Kitten	Lady
Bobcat	Falcon	Bulldog
Bronco	Seahawk	Pirate
Marlin	Panther	Buccaneer
Cavalier	Ram	Penguin
Jaguar	Star	Thunder
Rebel	Lightning	Saint

WHAT'S YOUR MASCOT?

School name: _____

Mascot: _____

DRAW IT HERE:

BUMBLE BOY TO THE RESCUE!

Ms. Clarke isn't the only English-language expert! Check out Mrs. Hickson's lesson below, then turn the page for an awesome Mad Lib!

EXAMPLES:
Bumble Boy (person),
beehive hideaway (place),
honey (thing)

EXAMPLES:
fly,
sting,
buzz

An adjective is a word that describes a noun.

EXAMPLES:
super (describes Bumble Boy),
evil (describes a villain),
scared (describes innocent villagers)

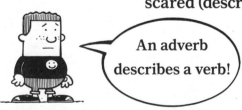

An adverb describes a verb!

AN EXAMPLE OF AN ADVERB IN A SENTENCE:
Nate thinks Bumble Boy acts <u>heroically</u> all the time!

MAKE A LIST OF THE SILLIEST
WORDS YOU CAN THINK OF:

1. Noun:

2. Verb (past tense):

3. Noun:

4. Adjective:

5. Noun:

6. Noun:

7. Verb (past tense):

8. Noun:

9. Adjective:

10. Noun:

NOW TURN THE PAGE

AND USE YOUR LIST

TO FILL IN THE BLANKS!

One of Nate's favorite comic heroes is the one and only Bumble Boy! Fill in the blanks and help create his next adventure.

Bumble Boy was buzzing along when a gigantic

_____ stood in his way. Bumble Boy
    1.

_____ fast and began flapping his wings.
    2.

The people of _____ were afraid that the
                    3.

evil villain named _____ _____
                        4.   5.

might destroy them all with his awful _____
                                            6.

and set fire to the city.

        Then Bumble Boy _____ his secret
                                7.

weapon, a _____ , and turned his enemy
                8.

to a _____ _____ , and all were
        9.   10.

saved!

...BUT THEN
BUMBLE BOY
CAME TO
THE RESCUE!

CLUB CENTRAL

According to Nate,
who should be in the
greatest club ever?

START

FINISH

WELCOME, DOODLERS!

NEVER FAIL SALES

Check out these advertisements for super-cool toys. Then draw your own ads for them! Be a stellar salesperson like Nate and his rival, Artur!

SLOGAN: GET OUT OF THIS WORLD!

SLOGAN:

CUSTOMIZED
SKATEBOARD!

HI-FLYIN'

YOUR NAME!

YOUR ART!

- 55mm wheels
- cast aluminum truck assembly

YOU DESIGN THE BOARD YOU WANT!

SLOGAN: _____

...BUT **I'LL** CONVINCE PEOPLE TO BUY 'EM!...

...ONCE I TURN ON THE OL' NATE WRIGHT CHARM!

DARE TO BE DORKY

**Check out Nate's Dorkiness Hall of Fame—
who would make your list?**

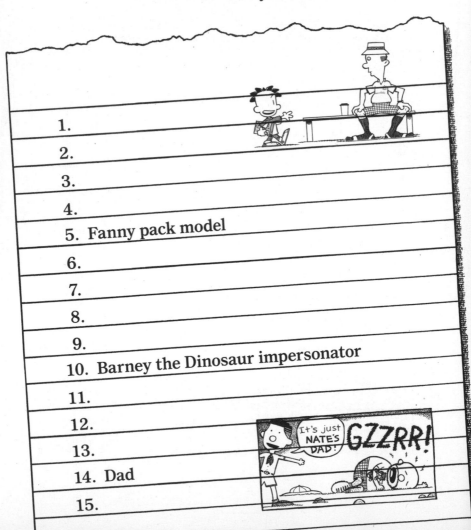

1.
2.
3.
4.
5. Fanny pack model
6.
7.
8.
9.
10. Barney the Dinosaur impersonator
11.
12.
13.
14. Dad
15.

16.

17.

18. The teacher's pet

19.

20.

21.

22.

23. Polka dance instructor

24.

25.

26.

27.

28.

29.

30.

the DORKINESS HALL of FAME

| Star Trek groupie | Poodle stylist | Hall monitor | Annoying classmate |

TO SCRIBBLE, OR NOT

It's that time again—scribble time!

Add your caption here:

NOT AGAIN!

Nate's used to embarrassing situations, like when his locker exploded! Using the letters in the word "embarrassing," see how many other words you can create!

EMBARRASSING

1.   16.

2.   17.

3.   18.

4.   19.

5.   20.

6.   21.

7.   22.

8.   23.

9.   24.

10.   25.

11.   26.

12.

13.

14.

15.

DISGUISE MASTER

What's Nate's secret identity? See if you can fill in the grid so that each disguise letter appears once in each column, row, and box.

 B = **BATMAN**

S = **SCOUT**

 H = **HULA DANCER**

P = **POET**

DROOL-A-THON

Nate's dad is the king of nutrition. Solve the clues and find out what Nate would rather be eating!

ACROSS

3. Little and frosted with sprinkles—perfect for birthdays!

6. Dark, milk, bittersweet—it's the best treat around.

8. Served in a bun. Not cold but _____. Not a cat but a _____.

10. Mmmm, nice and meaty and comes from a cow.

12. Fizzy, bubbly, sometimes called pop.

13. First word: a farmyard bird that clucks. Second word: there are five of these on your hand.

14. Pick up a slice of _____ pizza!

DOWN

1. Gooey noodle dish.

2. A Mexican treat that comes in a shell, crispy or soft.

4. This is much better with meatballs!

5. You scream, I scream, we all scream for _____.

7. Nate goes nuts for these.

9. First word rhymes with "merry." Second word: Nate threw this at Randy once!

11. Perfect for the movies, with extra butter.

COMIC RELIEF

Laugh attack! Teddy loves to joke around! Find out the punch lines to his jokes by using his secret code.

A	B	C	D	E	F	G	H	I	J	K	L	M
Z	Y	X	W	V	U	T	S	R	Q	P	O	N

N	O	P	Q	R	S	T	U	V	W	X	Y	Z
M	L	K	J	I	H	G	F	E	D	C	B	A

Q: What did the outlaw get when he stole a calendar?

A: __ __ __ __ __ __
    G D V O E V

   __ __ __ __ __ __ .
   N L M G S H

Q: Have you heard about the restaurant on the moon?

A: _ _ _ _ _
T I V Z G

_ _ _ _ _ _ _
U L L W   Y F G

_ _   _ _ _ _ _ _ _ _ _ _ .
M L   Z G N L H K S V I V

SNICKER!

Q: Why couldn't the sailors play cards?

A: _ _ _ _ _ _ _   _ _ _
Y V X Z F H V   G S V

_ _ _ _ _ _ _   _ _ _
X Z K G Z R M   D Z H

_ _ _ _ _ _ _ _   _ _
H G Z M W R M T   L M

_ _ _
G S V

_ _ _ _ .
W V X P

HA HA   HEH HEH   HA HA HA   HA

ARTUR, THE PERFECT

It looks like annoyingly perfect Artur is outselling Nate.
Fill in the speech balloons and decide what happens!

ON THE SPOT

Quick! It's quiz time. Find out if you are a BIG NATE expert extraordinaire.

1. Which Timber Scout's dad is the troop leader?

a. Nate

b. Artur

c. Teddy

d. Francis

e. Chad

2. Which P.S. 38 faculty member oversees detention?

a. Coach John

b. Ms. Clarke

c. Mrs. Czerwicki

d. Mr. Staples

e. Mr. Rosa

3. Choose the merit badge Nate DOES NOT want to earn:

a. Attendance

b. Knot Tying

c. Tap Dancing

d. Public Speaking

e. Citizenship

4. Who does Nate think will be an <u>awesome</u> doodler?

a. Jenny

b. Francis

c. Gina

d. Ellen

e. Dee Dee

5. A rumor goes around school saying that Nate is in love with _____ .

...ROMEO!

YEAH, **LOVE BUNNY!**

a. Mrs. Godfrey

b. Himself

c. Jenny

d. Gina

e. Lee Ann Pfister

ARCHRIVALS

How can P.S. 38 compete with Jefferson?

LAP OF LUXURY

Nate's rival school, Jefferson, has a state-of-the-art rec room with a Ping-Pong table!

A PING-PONG table! A VENDING MACHINE!.... with CHEEZ DOODLES!

LIST THE COOL THINGS YOU WISH YOU HAD AT YOUR SCHOOL:

1. Video game station
2.
3.
4.
5.
6.
7. An ice-skating rink
8.
9.
10. Make your own s'more bar

GOLD-PLATED TOILETS!

⊕☻⊕⊕☻ !

All that's missing is the POPCORN! funky feet

FACT #2 The auditorium has movie-style seats and they RECLINE!

11.

12. A Slip 'N Slide in the gym

13.

14.

15.

16. Snow cone machine

17.

18.

19. Beanbag chairs in class

20.

21.

22.

23.

24.

25.

WHAT SMELLS?

Eww . . . Nate's school, P.S. 38, is filled with stinky smells like Mrs. Godfrey's breath!

RANK THE STANK!

RANK THESE OUTRAGEOUS ODORS FROM GROSS (1) TO GAG-A-THON (10)!

1. Randy's sweaty soccer socks _____

2. Gina's grape gum ball hair spray _____

3. Chad's concert of burps _____

4. Cafetorium meat loaf surprise _____

5. Mrs. Czerwicki's Love Dove perfume _____

6. Francis's mom's tuna-onion casserole _____

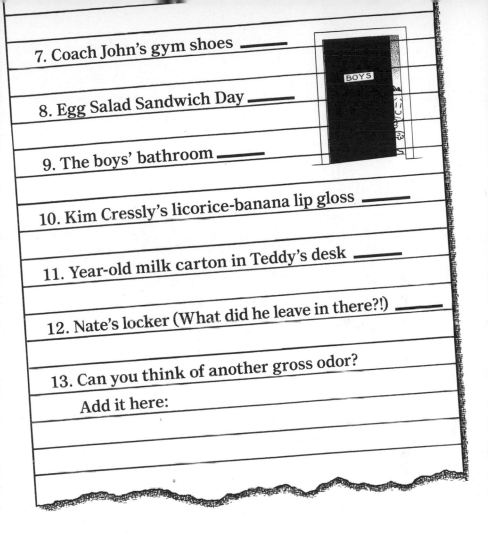

7. Coach John's gym shoes _____

8. Egg Salad Sandwich Day _____

9. The boys' bathroom _____

BOYS

10. Kim Cressly's licorice-banana lip gloss _____

11. Year-old milk carton in Teddy's desk _____

12. Nate's locker (What did he leave in there?!) _____

13. Can you think of another gross odor?

Add it here: _____

The mysterious air vent in Room 216!

YOU look in there.

No, YOU look in there.

SCHOOL SPIRIT

Unscramble the letters to uncover the mascot! Like this one ➡️

NOW YOU TRY!

V C A R A L E I

HINT: the rest are animals.

G I T S R E

O L I S N

_____

S E G L A E

_____

A S B E R

_____

L S L U B

_____

M S R A

_____

47

MYTH MADNESS

Nate is an Achilles expert! Can you fill in the grid so that each mythological figure shows up in every box, row, and column?

Z = **ZEUS**

H = **HADES**

A = **ACHILLES**

P = **POSEIDEN**

C = **CENTAUR**

M = **MEDUSA**

DANCE FEVER

What's your signature move? At P.S. 38, Nate goes to the Beach Party Dance, where there are some seriously snazzy dance moves, and it's NOT Mr. Staples's Robot. . . .

FACULTY CHAPERONES
Nothing says "awkward" like a math teacher doing the "Robot."
Hey, you guys, look at Mr. Staples!
Is that the "Robot" or the "Frankenstein"?

MIX AND MATCH WORDS AND MAKE UP CRAZY NEW DANCES!

Wild	Master	Turkey
Waterfall	Cat	Jam
Crawl	Trot	Blender
Chicken	Hustle	Electric
Bounce	Goose	Shopping Cart
Flash	Sprinkler	Monkey
Bunny	Slide	Hop
Jump	Loose	Zebra
Monster	Worm	Walk
Splash	Potato	Mash

WRITE YOUR
NEW DANCE MOVES HERE:

_____

_____   Turkey   Jam

_____

_____

Electric   Blender   _____

_____

_____   _____   Hop

_____   _____

_____   Chicken   Crawl

CARTOONING CLUB

Are you into drawing like Nate or Dee Dee? Nate's the president of P.S. 38's cartooning club. Can you copy each drawing below?

BACK TO NATURE

Francis, Nate, and their whole Timber Scout troop are headed into the great outdoors! Using Francis's secret code on page 10, find out the answers.

Q: **What taste are cats unable to detect?**

A: $\overline{24}$ $\overline{22}$ $\overline{8}$ $\overline{8}$ $\overline{6}$.

Q: **What living organism can be 30 times the size of a blue whale?**

A: $\overline{13}$ $\overline{3}$ $\overline{20}$ $\overline{13}$ $\overline{21}$ $\overline{6}$

$\overline{24}$ $\overline{8}$ $\overline{15}$ $\overline{10}$ $\overline{11}$ $\overline{20}$ $\overline{13}$ $\overline{6}$ $\overline{14}$ $\overline{8}$ $\overline{8}$.

WHO NEEDS TO SCRIBBLE?

You do! Take the time to transform this scribble.

Think up a great caption:

MIX-AND-MATCH MAYHEM

Match each character with the descriptions below!

A.

1.
A LOOOONG NECK!

B.

2.
ELEPHANT EARS!

C.

3.
BIG, BUGGY EYES!

D.

4.
A HANDLEBAR MUSTACHE!

E.

5.
A MISSING TOOTH!

OF **COURSE** THEY'RE FUNNY! THEY'RE NATE WRIGHT *ORIGINALS!*

Now be a cartoonist like Nate.
Use all 5 of these descriptions
to create YOUR own original character below!

MOMENTS OF GENIUS

List your all-time GREATEST genius moments!
C'mon, Nate knows he's brilliant, and so do you!

1.

2.

3.

4.

5. Dipping your chocolate bar into a jar of
   peanut butter

6.

7. Turning a cafeteria tray
   into a sled

8. Inventing your own time zone so you're
   never late!

SOUNDS LIKE A GREAT IDEA!

9.

10.

11. Convincing your little brother to do all
    your chores for one bag of Cheez Doodles

12.

YOU CAN'T RUSH **GENIUS!**

13.

14.

15. Having macaroni and cheese for breakfast

NOW **THAT'S** GREATNESS!

GROWN-UP GOSSIP

Oh no! What are these grown-ups talking about?? It definitely doesn't look good! Finish these comix by filling in the speech bubbles (use the semaphore code below).

CODE CHART	Use this alphabet to decode the secret messages in this book!	

⊡ = A	▯ = E	▽ = I	◖ = M	⊠ = Q	◎ = W
▭ = B	⊠ = F	◪ = J	◣ = N	⊞ = R	◨ = X
◿ = C	⊗ = G	◻ = K	⊞ = O	⊡ = S	■ = Y
◙ = D	▭ = H	▬ = L	▮ = P	◆ = T	⊠ = Z

Also: ▯▯ = U, ▭◼ = V

FAINT!

CJ

TRASH

CALLING ALL
CARTOONISTS

Who is going to join the Doodlers club?

START   **FINISH**

TOGETHERVILLE

Nate's had a crush on Jenny since 2nd grade, but she's in love with Artur. Poor Nate! Draw lines between the characters and make some perfect matches!

1.

2.

3.

4.

5.

A.

B.

C.

D.

E.

AWESOME ADD-ONS

To liven up the Jefferson CIC meeting, Nate and his friends play Add-On with the elements below! Fill in the grid so that each appears once in every column, row, and box.

 H = **HANDLEBAR MUSTACHE**

 T = **TAIL**

 E = **ELEPHANT EARS**

 S = **SOMBRERO**

 B = **BIG, BUGGY EYES**

 L = **LONG NECK**

 M = **MISSING TOOTH**

 D = **DUCK FOOT**

 R = **ROBOTIC ARM**

THIS IS **GUARANTEED** TO CRACK HIM UP!

GRAND-PRIZE JAMBOREE

At Nate's scout troop jamboree, he wins the GRAND PRIZE for selling the most Warm Fuzzies—an awesome customized skateboard! What would YOUR ultimate prize be?

RANK THESE FROM 1 TO 20.
20 = ÜBER-AWESOME.

_____ Tickets to a World Series

_____ A puppy

_____ Trip to Disney World

_____ Rollerblades

_____ Autographed baseball cards

_____ Gum ball machine

_____ Movie tickets for you and all your friends

_____ Super-cool sneakers

_____ The newest video game

_____ Cheeseburger and curly fries

_____ A basketball hoop for your driveway

_____ Haunted house tour

_____ Giant teddy bear

_____ Dance party

_____ Year-long bowling passes

_____ Dinner with the celebrity you love the most

_____ A digital camera

_____ Meeting with your favorite author

_____ Weekend at a water park

_____ Chocolate milk shake

_____ Personalized bike

_____ Drum set

THE ULTIMATE ULTRA-NATE!

Will Nate save Dee Dee from serious drama?
Fill in the speech bubbles and finish the scene!

GROUNDED!

Oh boy, Nate's in trouble, BIG time! List all the possible things Nate might be grounded for.

1.

2. Having an indoor fleeceball tournament in the house

3.

4.

5. Stealing Ellen's journal and passing the pages out to the 6th grade

6.

7.

8. Selling comix at the mall

9.

10.

YARD SALE SCRAMBLE

Nate brakes for yard sales. It's the best way to find classic comic books! Locate all 20 items in this super word scramble so that Nate finds his favorite comic, "BUMBLE BOY"!

ROLLERBLADES

TENNIS RACKET

SNOW GLOBE

GARDEN GNOME

WELCOME MAT

BASKETBALL

SUNGLASSES

CERAMIC KITTEN

COMIC BOOKS

LAWN CHAIR

BOARD GAME

FRISBEE

GOLF CLUBS

GLOVES

BINOCULARS

UMBRELLA

FRUIT BOWL

VASE

POSTER

SANDALS

COMIX DRAMA

What has Nate found? Treasure or trash?

Fill in the bubbles!

SUPER SCRIBBLE

Turn this scribble into something amazing!

Write your caption here:

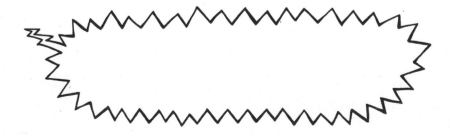

MOVE OVER, DR. DOLITTLE

Francis is an ace when it comes to animal knowledge. Use his code on page 10 to find out these cool facts.

$$\overline{26}\ \overline{13}\ \overline{18}\ \overline{8}\ \overline{23}\ \overline{24}$$

$$\overline{1}\ \overline{13}\ \overline{19}\ \overline{8}\qquad\overline{6}\ \overline{1}\ \overline{14}\ \overline{8}\ \overline{8}$$

$$\overline{8}\ \overline{9}\ \overline{8}\ \overline{23}\ \overline{20}\ \overline{25}\ \overline{24}.$$

$\overline{1}\ \overline{11}\ \overline{14}\ \overline{24}\ \overline{8}\ \overline{24}$

$\overline{26}\ \overline{13}\ \overline{21}\ \overline{21}\ \overline{11}\ \overline{6}$

$\overline{19}\ \overline{11}\ \overline{18}\ \overline{20}\ \overline{6}$.

$\overline{3}\ \overline{11}\ \overline{13}\ \overline{6}\ \overline{24},\quad \overline{8}\ \overline{9}\ \overline{8}\ \overline{24}$

$\overline{1}\ \overline{13}\ \overline{19}\ \overline{8}$

$\overline{14}\ \overline{8}\ \overline{26}\ \overline{6}\ \overline{13}\ \overline{21}\ \overline{3}\ \overline{10}\ \overline{23}\ \overline{13}\ \overline{14}$

$\overline{2}\ \overline{10}\ \overline{2}\ \overline{20}\ \overline{23}\ \overline{24}$.

WORST INJURIES EVER

...THERE ARE **GOOD** ONES AND **BAD** ONES!

Do you hate getting hurt, especially in an embarrassing way? Join Nate's club!

RANK THESE INSANE INJURIES FROM 1 TO 10. 10 = ÜBER-AWFUL.

1. Slipping in cat vomit and twisting your ankle _____

2. Falling off your bike in front of your crush _____

GROAN

3. Diving off a skateboard and landing in your neighbor's trash can _____

4. Getting a black eye because you mistakenly ran into a wall _____

5. Stepping in dog poop ____

6. Breaking your leg before
   the big basketball game ____

7. Landing flat on your face in the play ____

8. Getting a huge scratch from
   your hamster, Fluffy ____

9. Food allergy that makes you
   itchy all over ____

10. Write your worst injury here: ____

____

____

DREAM SCHOOL

Check out Jefferson's awesome school building!

What would your dream school look like? Draw it!

MODEL
TIMBER SCOUT

Nate is shocked when he learns who
used to be a Timber Scout!

FINISH

START

SURF'S UP!

If your school had a beach-themed dance, what would complete YOUR costume? Find all 20 beach accessories!

FLIP-FLOPS

SUNGLASSES

GRASS SKIRT

TANK TOP

SHORTS

SARONG

SHELL NECKLACE

HAWAIIAN SHIRT

VISOR

BEACH BALL

SURFBOARD

FLIPPERS

SNORKEL

SANDALS

INNER TUBE

TOWEL

FLOATIES

SUNBLOCK

GOGGLES

SWIM CAP

```
S D V N S E I T A O L F S A
V T A N K T O P O A L L E S
I T R I H S N A I I A W A H
S W E I L E W O T D B H S E
O A S D K S R S N P H K G L
R F R P R S S A K F C S D L
G A E O O A S E I O A L B N
S S P P N L O S L D E E I E
H L P L F G F B A G B K K C
O P I K U N N P F R G R B K
R F L E P U E R I R G O E L
T L F H S S P L D L U N G A
S W I M C A P P V S F S P C
F O A A D I N N E R T U B E
```

GRASS, **SHMASS!** I CAN'T BE SEEN IN **THIS!**

OH, COME **ON!** MEN IN HAWAII WEAR THEM **ALL THE TIME!**

PRINCIPAL'S POP QUIZ!

1. Who does Nate go to the school dance with?

a. Gina

b. Francis

c. Dee Dee

d. Jenny

HEY, EVERYONE! GUESS WHAT **NATE** JUST ASKED ME!

2. Who's the biggest bully of all?

a. Ellen

b. Randy

c. Coach John

d. Nolan

HE SAYS IT'S **PAYBACK TIME!**

3. Why does P.S. 38 close temporarily?

a. A fire

b. Mice

c. Mold

d. Nate got too many

detentions

P.S. 38 IS GOING TO BE **CLOSED** FOR A WHILE!

4. What's the theme of the P.S. 38 dance?

a. Winter Wonderland

b. Peter Pan

c. Ben Franklin and Friends

d. Beach Party

5. Principal Nichols gave Nate detention for

a. Tickling

b. Green bean incident

c. Insolence

d.

SCRIBBLE MANIA

Turn this scribble into . . .

Add a caption!

ELIMINATION STATION

Cross out the word that DOES NOT describe . . .

NATE'S FLEECEBALL GAME:

Action-packed   Competitive   Yawn-a-thon

NATE'S SISTER, ELLEN:

Annoying   Shy   Bossy

DETENTION:

Boring   Dazzling   Terrible

THE CAFETORIUM:

Gross   Crowded   Fancy

DOODLERS:

Creative   Scary   Artistic

NATE'S RIVAL, ARTUR:

Perfect   Polite   Wild

SUPER-SAPPY PET NAMES

Nate can't stand ooey-gooey, lovey-dovey pet names like Dumpling Face and Puffy Bunny. Mix and match the words below to make the silliest pet names!

Huggy	Pooky	Lily
Princess	Posey	Cookie
Puddles	Sweetie	Kitty
Pie	Silly	Buttercup
Dove	Precious	Bear
Pumpkin	Candy	Rosy
Baby	Lovey	Pea
Bug	Pretty	Bunny
Pudding	Sugar	Cakes
Cutie	Funny	Face
Cuddle	Doll	Muffin

LIST YOUR
SUPER-SAPPY PET NAME
CREATIONS HERE!

Cuddle   Cookie   Cakes

Funny   Bunny   Face

CRAZIEST COSTUMES

Nate once wore a hula skirt to the school dance! List the top 20 craziest costumes ever, then grade them from A to F. A = Awesome!

COSTUME	GRADE
1.	——
2.	——
3. Caveman	——
4.	——
5.	——
6. Cow	——
7.	——

I call it a "wheel."

OOOH!

MOOOO

COSTUME	GRADE
8.	——
9. Lobster	——
10.	——
11.	——
12.	——
13.	——
14.	——
15. The planet Venus	——
16.	——
17.	——
18.	——
19.	——
20.	——

SO... WHERE'D YOU GET THIS THING, ANYWAY?

RUSTLE RUSTLE

PFFFT!

Oh, brother.

WHAT'S THE S████P?

You decide the news! Pretend you're a reporter and fill in the speech bubbles!

BE TRUE TO YOUR SCHOOL

Mix and match! Do these things belong at P.S. 38 or Jefferson Middle School?

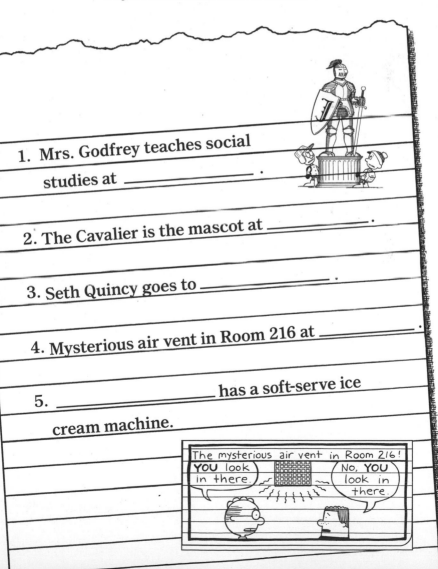

1. Mrs. Godfrey teaches social studies at _____ .

2. The Cavalier is the mascot at _____ .

3. Seth Quincy goes to _____ .

4. Mysterious air vent in Room 216 at _____ .

5. _____ has a soft-serve ice cream machine.

> The mysterious air vent in Room 216!
>
> YOU look in there.
>
> No, YOU look in there.

THE DOODLER

Nate's the president of P.S. 38's cartooning club, aka the Doodlers. Can YOU doodle? Go for it!

DONUT DREAMS

NARF
NARF
NUMF

Nate's dad never has yummy snacks at home, only lame ones like rice cakes! So Nate loves sweet treats, like donuts.

MIX AND MATCH ITEMS FROM
LISTS A AND B TO MAKE
THE PERFECT DONUT!

Not THAT kind of donut!

honey glazed

SPLURCH!

LIST A

Maple

Coconut

Strawberry

Cherry

Jelly

Blueberry

Vanilla

Rainbow sprinkles

Honey

LIST B

Chocolate

Cream

Lemon

Glazed

Raspberry

Peanut butter

Fudge

M&Ms

Marshmallow

DRAMA-RAMA

Dee Dee loves drama! Draw what happens after each Dee Dee scene.

LUNCH

I'M *BLEEDING!*

I feel faint... getting weak... weaker...

I'LL CALL AN *AMBULANCE!*

NOTORIOUS NAMES

Using the letters in each character's name below, write down cool adjectives (see the definition on page 22) or phrases that describe them.

ROWDY

A _____

N _____

D _____

Y _____

N _____

O _____

L _____

A _____

NASTY

C _____

HAPPY

A _____

D _____

M_____

R._____

R_____

O_____

S_____

ARTISTIC

D_____

E_____

E_____

DRAMATIC

E_____

E_____

C_____

O_____

A_____

C_____

H_____

JOCK

O_____

H_____

N_____

COMIX MASH-UP!

What happens when these wacky characters meet on the street? Draw it!

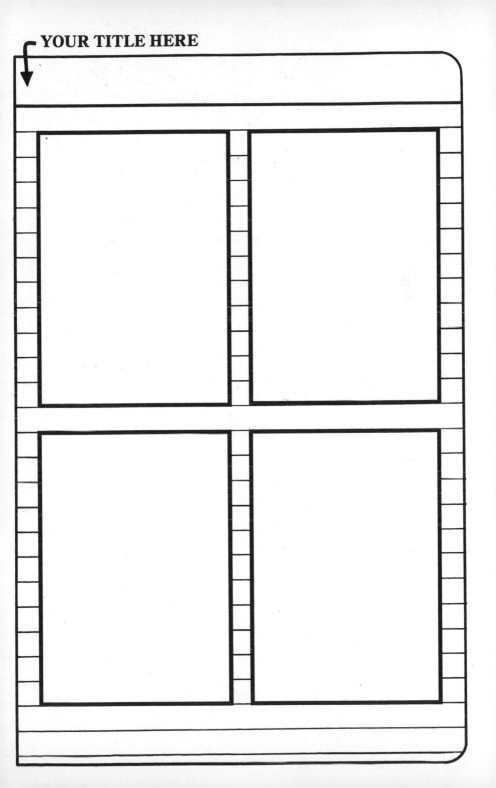

YOUR TITLE HERE

BIG NATE TRIVIA BONANZA

For each incident described,
write the Big Nate book it appeared in!

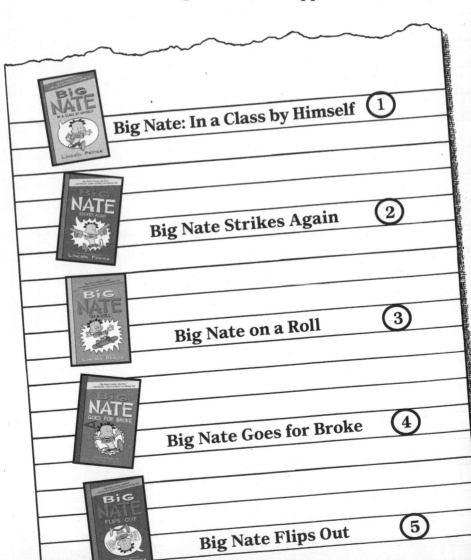

Big Nate: In a Class by Himself ①

Big Nate Strikes Again ②

Big Nate on a Roll ③

Big Nate Goes for Broke ④

Big Nate Flips Out ⑤

Nate's a team captain. ②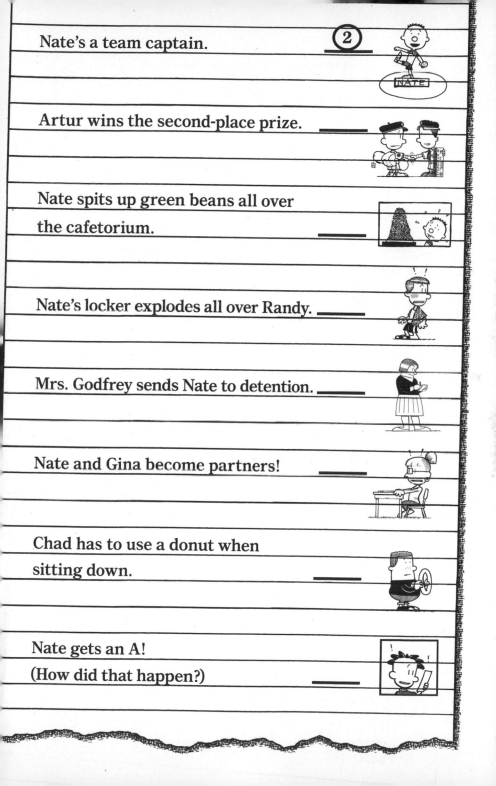

Artur wins the second-place prize. ____

Nate spits up green beans all over
the cafetorium. ____

Nate's locker explodes all over Randy. ____

Mrs. Godfrey sends Nate to detention. ____

Nate and Gina become partners! ____

Chad has to use a donut when
sitting down. ____

Nate gets an A!
(How did that happen?) ____

ART ATTACK!

Nate's favorite things to do are draw, make comix, and doodle too! See if you can solve the puzzle and find all of Nate's art supplies!

ACROSS

3. When you make a mistake, this makes things disappear.

4. Often #2 instead of #1. Yellow and rhymes with "stencil."

6. Rhymes with "faint." This can be watercolor or oil.

7. This is where Nate does his doodling in class! First half of the word rhymes with "goat"; second half rhymes with "hook."

DOWN

1. Not always for your hair, you can use this to create masterpieces!

2. A colorful drawing tool made out of wax!

5. You can use this to draw cool pictures on the sidewalk!

6. Nate's teacher Mr. Galvin once had a _____ stain on his shirt pocket.

WHAT HAPPENS NEXT?

Watch out, this looks like trouble! You decide what's going on and finish the next frame, using the code on page 12.

_____

_____

_____

_____

_____

_____

⊕⊕, ◑⊕⊕
◐⊕⊕⊕⊕!

_____

_____

◑⊕⊕◑
⊕◑◐⊕⊕!

_____

_____

LOVE BUG

Nate's crush is Jenny. Too bad she's dating the annoyingly perfect Artur! List your <u>TOP 10</u> favorite people here (a rock star? your neighbor?).

1.

2.

3.

4.

5.

6.

7.

8.

9.

10.

STAND BACK, EVERYBODY! HERE COMES THE HOT NEW COUPLE!!

ADMISSION $5

DRAMA QUEEN

Who is the drama queen of P.S. 38?

CRAZY-CHARACTER QUIZ

Which of these Big Nate characters are you most like?

1. What's your favorite school club?

   a. The Doodlers cartooning club

   b. Drama Club

   c. Donut-Hole Appreciation Society

   d. Dodgeball

   e. Chess team

Not **THAT** kind of donut!

honey glazed

SPLURCH!

2. What food do you hate most?

   a. egg salad

   b. green beans (so not dramatic!)

   c. rice cakes

   d. coconut-yogurt pie

   e. Twinkies
   (you're too healthy for those!)

SIGH...

3. What are you most afraid of?

a. cats

b. neutral color schemes

c. yogurt

d. Nothing!

e. not getting perfect grades

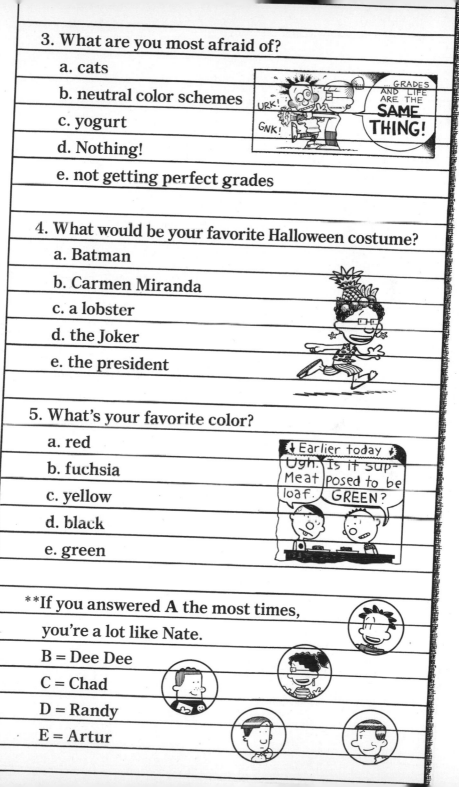

4. What would be your favorite Halloween costume?

a. Batman

b. Carmen Miranda

c. a lobster

d. the Joker

e. the president

5. What's your favorite color?

a. red

b. fuchsia

c. yellow

d. black

e. green

If you answered **A the most times, you're a lot like Nate.

B = Dee Dee

C = Chad

D = Randy

E = Artur

FRUITOPIA

Dee Dee's beach party headdress looked so appetizing, Chad couldn't help taking a bite! Fill in the grid so each fruit shows up once in the rows, columns, and boxes.

P = **PINEAPPLE**

O = **ORANGE**

G = **GRAPE**

B = **BANANAS**

DOWN WITH CAVALIERS!

P.S. 38's rival mascot is the cavalier. So annoying!
Using the letters in "cavaliers," see how many words
you can make!

PS: If you find 25 or more, you lead P.S. 38 to victory!

CAVALIERS

1.   16.
2.   17.
3. live   18.
4.   19. rival
5.   20.
6.   21.
7.   22.
8. evil   23.
9.   24.
10.   25.
11.   26.
12.
13.
14.
15.

SPEED SCRIBBLE!

Play the scribble game . . . in 10 seconds!

Don't forget the caption!

CHILL OUT!

What do you love to do when it's cold outside? Unscramble the letters to uncover these favorite activities for winter fun!

N G L S D E D I

_____

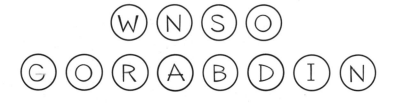

W N S O
G O R A B D I N

_____

_____

N W B O S L L A
T H I G F

_____

Ⓖ Ⓢ Ⓚ Ⓘ Ⓝ Ⓘ

_____

Ⓤ Ⓘ Ⓝ Ⓑ Ⓛ Ⓓ Ⓘ Ⓖ
Ⓐ Ⓜ Ⓝ Ⓐ Ⓝ Ⓢ Ⓦ Ⓞ

_____

_____

Ⓒ Ⓔ Ⓘ - Ⓚ Ⓐ Ⓣ Ⓢ Ⓝ Ⓖ Ⓘ

_____

Ⓡ Ⓝ Ⓓ Ⓘ Ⓝ Ⓚ Ⓘ Ⓖ
Ⓐ Ⓒ Ⓞ Ⓒ Ⓞ

_____

JOKING AROUND

Check out Teddy's super-silly jokes! Use the codes on pages 12 and 60 to find out the answers.

Q: What has eyes but cannot see?

A: ⊕ ⊕⊕⊕⊕⊕⊕ !

__ __ __ __ __ __ __ !

Q: What did the traffic light say to the car?

A: ⬡⬜◤'◇ ⬛⊞⬜ !
⬜'◖ ◸◼⬤◣◺◹◺◿ !

__ __ __ , __ __ __ __ __ !

__ ' __ __ __ __ __ __ __ __ !

Q: What did one wall say to the other wall?

A: ⬚⬚⬚⬚ ⬚⬚ ⬚⬚ ⬚⬚⬚ ⬚⬚⬚⬚⬚⬚!

_ _ _ _   _ _ _ _

_ _ _   _ _ _ _ _ _ !

Q: What has teeth but cannot eat?

A: ⊕ ⊕⊕⊕⊕ !

_   _ _ _ _ _ !

Q: Why did the dog stay in the shade?

A: ⬚⬚ ⬚⬚⬚ ⬚⬚⬚ ⬚⬚⬚⬚ ⬚⬚ ⬚⬚ ⬚ ⬚⬚⬚ ⬚⬚⬚!

_ _   _ _ _   _ _ _   _ _ _ _

_ _   _ _ _   _   _ _ _   _ _ _ !

CREATE-A-CHARACTER

Come up with your own character
like Nate and Dee Dee.

**ANSWER THE FOLLOWING QUESTIONS
ABOUT YOUR CHARACTER:**

1. What does his/her laugh sound like?

2. What kind of costume/outfit does he/she wear?
   Does he/she have a hat or cape?

3. Is he/she evil, good, fun, wild, wacky, smart, silly?

DOCTOR CESSPOOL, YOU'RE A GENIUS!

by N.W. THE END by D.D.H.

4. What does his/her hair look like?

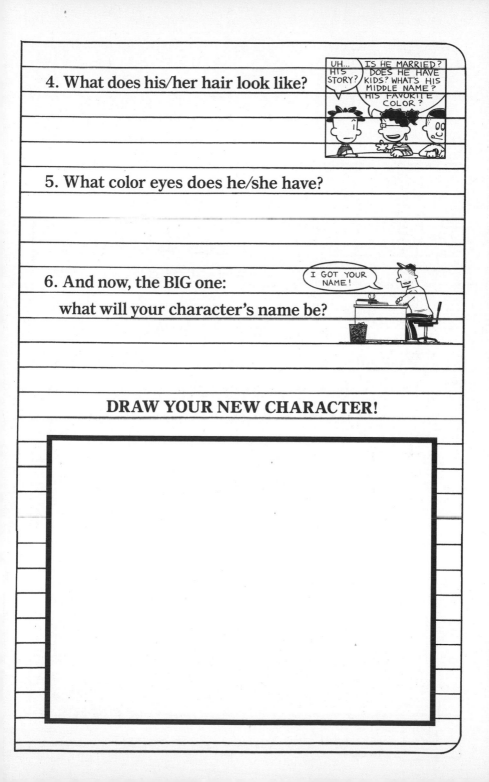

5. What color eyes does he/she have?

6. And now, the BIG one:

what will your character's name be?

DRAW YOUR NEW CHARACTER!

LUCKY BREAK

Circle which moments you think are the luckiest!

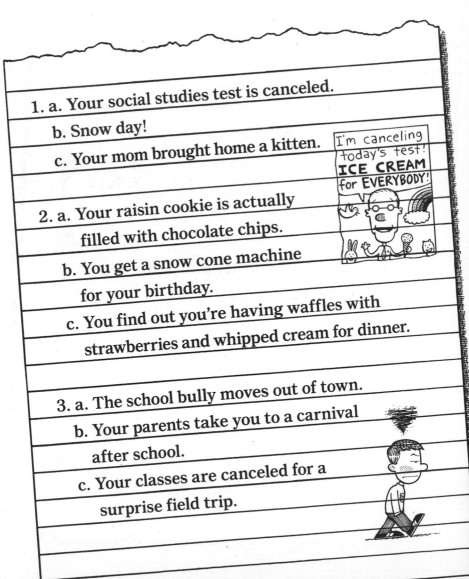

1. a. Your social studies test is canceled.

   b. Snow day!

   c. Your mom brought home a kitten.

2. a. Your raisin cookie is actually filled with chocolate chips.

   b. You get a snow cone machine for your birthday.

   c. You find out you're having waffles with strawberries and whipped cream for dinner.

3. a. The school bully moves out of town.

   b. Your parents take you to a carnival after school.

   c. Your classes are canceled for a surprise field trip.

NOW LIST YOUR TOP 10 LUCKIEST MOMENTS!!

1.

2.

3.

4.

5. You get an A++ on your end-of-year report.

6.

7.

8. A water park is built near your house.

9.

10.

CRAZY FOR CODES!

Create your very own <u>secret</u> <u>code</u>, just like the one Nate and his friend Francis have. Draw a symbol for each letter in the alphabet.

A = ◆

B =

C =

D = //

E =

F =

G = }

H =

I =

J = ●

K =

L =

M = ◎

N =

O = ⌐

P = ⬆

Q = ●●●

R =

S = |||

T = ∧∧

U =

V =

W = ▭

X =

Y =

Z =

PRACTICE YOUR CODE—
WRITE THE FOLLOWING
SENTENCES IN YOUR
NEW ALPHABET!

N A T E   I S   O N E

_ ◆ ∧ _   _ ||| ⌐ _ _

F U N N Y   G U Y.

_ _ _ _ ≥ _ _ _ .

T H E   B O B C A T   I S

∧ _ _   _ ⌐ _ _ ◆ ∧   _ |||

A   C O O L

◆   _ ⌐ ⌐ _

M A S C O T.

◎ ◆ ||| _ ⌐ ∧ .

CONSTRUCTION JUNCTION

When Nate's school is closed for repairs, Dee Dee's dad, the construction worker, is on the job! See if you can find all the construction tools and equipment in the puzzle.

HARD HAT

BULLDOZER

LADDER

TRAFFIC CONE

SCREWDRIVER

SHOVEL

CHISEL

WRENCH

HANDSAW

TOOL BELT

FORKLIFT

EXCAVATOR

DUMP TRUCK

CHERRY PICKER

CRANE

DRILL

BACKHOE LOADER

MEASURING TAPE

```
U A R H T F I L K R O F E R H
A P K R H O E T D E W E B E L
L N C E E A O R L R A X A O N
C E U D N D F L E E T C R H L
P E R A L O I N B R H A E T R
R A T O H R C L V E R V D T I
B D P L D H E C R N L A D E R
U L M E A S U R I N G T A P E
L K U O I R Y H H F H O L W L
L S D H E P W A C A F R L I C
D V C K I C I N R C F A D U E
O A S C R E W D R I V E R C A
Z A K A K N H S H O V E L T E
E E N B H A C A T E D A I E C
R E S I T F I W B S O D I L K
```

MESS ALERT!

Nate is one messy guy! Just take a look at his exploding locker!! Make him feel better and list your TOP TEN messes. YUCK!

1.

2.

3.

4. Getting peanut butter in
   my hair

5.

REWIND!

What happened right before each
dramatic moment? You draw it!

ROCK ON!

It's time for the school of rock! If you can solve the puzzle, Nate's band will have a killer show!

ACROSS

1. A _____ focuses on the performers, creating a bright circle.

3. Groove to the _____. Hint: Starts with "m."

4. Groupies go wild when the show starts! Rhymes with "cans."

6. Nate plays these! Rhymes with "thumbs."

8. The whole group of performers. Rhymes with "hand."

9. We got the _____. Rhymes with "heat"!

DOWN

1. This person uses the microphone.

2. A cool instrument with strings!

5. When only one of the group performs, it's called a _____. Rhymes with "polo"!

7. Platform where the magic happens! Rhymes with "rage."

CRAZY ADD-ON!

Nate and his cartooning club, the Doodlers, love to play Add-On. Add each of the things on the list below to your drawing!

1. A PEG LEG

2. SOMBRERO

3. A LEI

4. A SKATEBOARD

5. STRIPED SHIRT

6. ONE WEBBED FOOT

7. GRASS SKIRT

8. MITTENS

9. CHEEZ DOODLES

10. PICKLES THE CAT

GAWK!

LAUGH-O-METER

What tickles <u>your</u> funny bone?

Rank these things on the laugh-o-meter!

OUT OF CONTROL

BELLY LAUGH

CHUCKLES

GIGGLES

WA HA HA HA
OH HO
HO HO
HA HA

The school principal is dressed as the mascot!

☐ OUT OF CONTROL ☐ BELLY LAUGH

☐ CHUCKLES ☐ GIGGLES

Your mom burps (<u>really</u> loud) by accident at the grocery store.

☐ OUT OF CONTROL ☐ BELLY LAUGH

☐ CHUCKLES ☐ GIGGLES

Your science teacher spits when he talks.

☐ OUT OF CONTROL ☐ BELLY LAUGH

☐ CHUCKLES ☐ GIGGLES

The neighbor's dog is wearing a mini top hat and cape.

☐ OUT OF CONTROL ☐ BELLY LAUGH
☐ CHUCKLES ☐ GIGGLES

The mall cop sings "You Are My Sunshine" at the top of his lungs.

☐ OUT OF CONTROL ☐ BELLY LAUGH
☐ CHUCKLES ☐ GIGGLES

Your dad break-dances to hip-hop at a family wedding.

☐ OUT OF CONTROL ☐ BELLY LAUGH
☐ CHUCKLES ☐ GIGGLES

Mrs. Hickson throws up in the middle of Breakfast Book Club!

☐ OUT OF CONTROL ☐ BELLY LAUGH
☐ CHUCKLES ☐ GIGGLES

Your aunt has a crazy hairdo from the '80s.

☐ OUT OF CONTROL ☐ BELLY LAUGH
☐ CHUCKLES ☐ GIGGLES

CLUB BONANZA

P.S. 38 has tons of after-school clubs to join. Fill out the grid so that each club shows up once in each row, column, and box!

W = **WIZARDS & WITCHES**

K = **KNIT PICKERS**

B = **SCHOOL BEAUTIFICATION SOCIETY**

P = **PROBLEM SOLVERS**

S = **SPOTLIGHT CLUB**

D = **DOODLERS**

SPOTLIGHT ON...

K	W	B		D	
P			W	B	
		P			S
	B	K		W	
		K			
B		S	D		W

POSTER PASSION

Check out Dee Dee's
Beach Party
Dance poster!
Now it's your turn!
Draw your own
dance poster here. →

SUPER NATE, SUPER FAST

Can you answer these

Nate Wright questions in under 2 minutes?

1. Which one of these is <u>not</u> a Nate Wright original comic character?

a. Moe Mentum

b. Cosmic Cat

c. Dr. Cesspool

d. Ultra-Nate

e. Tish Dishley

2. In what ultimate competition does P.S. 38 go up against Jefferson?

a. fleeceball

b. chess tournament

c. tug of war

d. water balloon fight

e. snow sculpture contest

JEFFERSON ISN'T SO BAD **AFTER** ALL!

3. What kind of pet does Mr. Eustis have?

a. parakeet

b. ferret

c. rabbit

d. dog

e. hamster

4. Jefferson's cafetorium goes by this name . . .

a. meet 'n' eat

b. food court

c. snack station

d. dining hall

e. hungry haven

5. Nolan the bully ruins Teddy's favorite new toy—what is it?

a. Transformer

b. Supa-Sno Tube

c. telescope

d. teddy bear

e. Super Soaker water gun

DARE TO BE DEE DEE

When it comes to drama, Dee Dee is the queen!
Draw Dee Dee's face when each of these things happen.

**SHE'S STUNG
BY A BEE!**

**SHE PERFORMS IN THE
SCHOOL MUSICAL "GREASE."**

**SHE SEES CHAD FALL
ON THE PLAYGROUND.**

**SHE JOINS
THE DOODLERS.**

**SHE EATS
BRUSSELS SPROUTS.**

**SHE'S CAUGHT SPYING
ON RANDY.**

SCRIBBLE SENSATION!

Are you a scribble-game genius?

Don't forget the caption!

TICKLE YOUR FUNNY BONE

What's up with Nate?

Fill in the speech bubbles and a title for each!

YOUR TITLE: _____

YOUR TITLE: _____

DEAR NATE...

If you could write a letter to Nate, what would you say? <u>Try it!</u> He's waiting to hear from YOU.

Dear Nate,

I think you are VERY funny! I love to draw and doodle, too.

FRIENDS!!

Sincerely,

_____

(Sign your name here.)

DANCING QUEEN

Nate's school dance was a beach party. What would your ultimate dance party be called?

MAKE UP COOL NAMES BY DRAWING LINES FROM LIST A TO LISTS B AND C.

List A	List B	List C
Snowflake	Heart	Rock
Wild	Halloween	Hoedown
Pajama	Monster	Festival
Pirate	Fright	Fling
Country	Costume	Swing
Winter	Hay	Hop
Crazy	Jungle	Carnival
Blizzard	Underwater	Bop
Honkey-Tonk	Soul	Ball
Black-and-White	Smile	Party
Heaven	Silly	Bowl

WRITE YOUR AWESOME SCHOOL DANCE NAMES HERE!

_____

_____

__Wild__   __Fright__   __Festival__

_____

__Honkey-Tonk__   __Hay__   __Hop__

_____

_____

_____

_____

_____

ALL SHOOK UP!

Ready, set, WRITE! Unscramble the letters to find characters from Nate's world.

O N A L N

_____

R M .   P L A S S T E

_____

E D T D Y

_____

Y J N E N

_____

| E | L | L | N | E |

_____

| M | K | I | | R | E | C | L | S | Y | S |

_____

| N | F | A | S | I | R | C |

_____

| H | O | C | A | C | | H | J | N | O |

_____

| R | T | A | R | U |

_____

SNOWDOWN!

Instead of a throwdown, it's a snowdown! It's up to you to help P.S. 38 win the snow sculpture competition. Using the letters in the name "Achilles," how many other words can you make? If you find 25 words, you lead P.S. 38 to victory!

...WE NEED TO MAKE **EVERY SECOND COUNT!**

ACHILLES

1.

2.

3.

4.

5. lies

6.

7.

8.

9.

10. sale

11.

12.

13.

14.

15. sill

16.

17.

18.

19. case

20.

21.

22. chill

23.

24.

25.

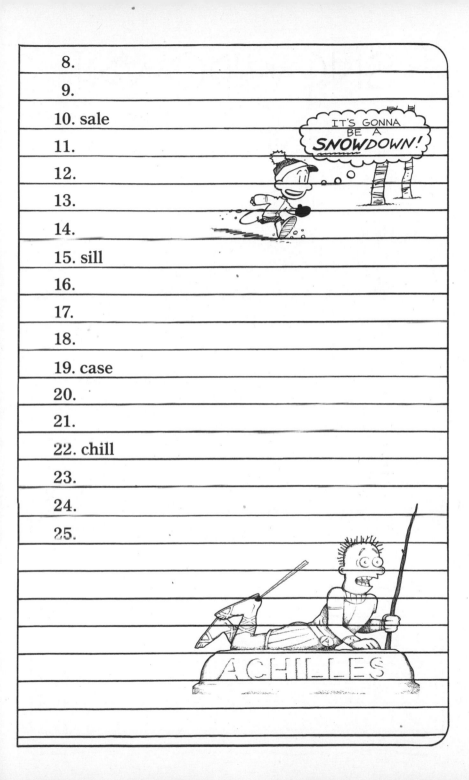

SPORTS SNAPSHOT

Do you remember the very first sport you ever played? Was it baseball, basketball, soccer, or volleyball? Nate's first sport was Little League baseball! Check it out!

DRAW YOURSELF PLAYING
YOUR VERY FIRST SPORT!

⊕⊕⊕ ⊕⊕⊕ ⊕⊕⊕⊕ ⊕⊕⊕?

YOUR ANSWER: _____

NOW DRAW YOUR BEST FRIEND PLAYING THE
SPORT HE OR SHE LOVES TO PLAY THE MOST!

ALOHA, HAWAIIAN TIME!

Nate's school dance has a beach party theme. Everyone dresses for the tropics, like wearing Hawaiian shirts. Design your own Hawaiian shirts here!

COOLEST-CLUB CHALLENGE

Nate is serious about chess AND the cartooning club. What's YOUR favorite club? See if you can find all the amazing club names in the puzzle.

SINGING SENSATION

RAP AND RHYMERS

MUSIC MASTERS

FUN PATROL

FACTASTIC FEW

SKATER BRIGADE

SCI-FI SCIONS

DREAM TEAM

BOOK BUNCH

COMMUNITY SERVICE CREW

MATHLETES

GYMNASTICS GROUP

GREAT GAMERS

ARTISTS ALLIANCE

KARAOKE CROONERS

BRAINIACS

THESPIANS

YEARBOOK COMMITTEE

CRAFT CLUB

HIP-HOP DANCE QUEENS

R	H	O	I	N	O	I	T	A	S	N	E	S	G	N	I	G	N	I	S
E	D	E	R	E	E	S	I	I	O	S	A	E	T	G	S	S	T	N	Y
F	S	B	F	B	K	N	R	P	A	E	I	N	S	N	P	R	E	N	S
N	R	C	A	Y	D	O	A	R	I	D	R	E	A	M	T	E	A	M	E
W	E	R	C	E	C	I	V	R	E	S	Y	T	I	N	U	M	M	O	C
N	N	A	T	A	E	C	S	R	T	G	C	V	G	Q	O	Y	F	C	N
S	O	F	A	R	O	S	N	H	M	Y	R	A	E	R	M	H	E	R	A
C	O	T	S	B	A	I	P	I	C	M	M	C	I	T	V	R	A	U	I
S	R	C	T	O	S	F	G	P	A	N	N	M	E	N	S	D	A	C	L
I	C	L	I	O	A	I	S	C	U	A	U	A	Y	A	I	N	C	T	L
C	E	U	C	K	A	C	E	R	D	S	I	B	R	I	M	A	E	I	A
G	K	B	F	C	P	S	F	P	I	T	N	F	K	B	R	P	R	R	S
T	O	A	E	O	R	T	O	C	E	I	K	T	E	O	E	A	R	B	T
S	A	R	W	M	T	H	M	B	E	C	I	H	G	U	O	R	R	Y	S
C	R	F	O	M	P	A	T	H	E	S	P	I	A	N	S	B	E	S	I
A	A	K	S	I	S	R	E	M	A	G	T	A	E	R	G	O	N	L	T
A	K	I	H	T	S	K	A	T	E	R	B	R	I	G	A	D	E	N	R
A	A	E	E	T	O	T	I	N	V	O	S	O	F	P	U	C	N	I	A
I	A	R	O	E	A	S	R	R	F	U	N	P	A	T	R	O	L	R	K
T	S	E	T	E	L	H	T	A	M	P	A	M	E	S	A	E	C	E	R

...AND HAVE **FUN** OUT THERE!

SUPER SNOW SCULPTOR

Nate, Francis, and Teddy are expert snowman sculptors! How about you? Design your ultimate snowmen: add outfits, eyes, mouths—anything you want!

INSIDER INFO

What are the secrets of Nate's world? Let's see if you know ALL of them!

1. What is Chad afraid of?

   a. cats

   b. scary movies

   c. yogurt

   d. the dark

   e. Gina

2. P.S. 38 wins the ultimate showdown with Jefferson by creating a sculpture of whom?

   a. Zeus

   b. Achilles

   c. Poseidon

   d. Caesar

   e. Mickey Mouse

ANYBODY CAN BE BEATEN!

3. Jefferson Middle School's mascot is . . .

a. a knight

b. a tiger

c. a bull

d. a cavalier

e. an elephant

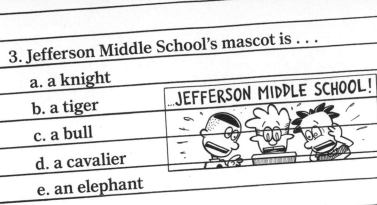

4. How does Nate hurt his wrist?

a. Hitting Randy on the playground

b. Playing fleeceball against Nolan

c. Trying to catch Chad's donut

d. Playing the drums too hard

e. Falling off his skateboard

NOTORIOUS NAMES ROUND TWO!

Check out Nate's super-cool name challenge! For each letter in these characters' names, write down an adjective (see page 22 for the definition) or phrase that describes the person, beginning with that letter!

S_____

PICKLES'S FRIEND

I _____

T_____

S_____

Y_____

HOW DOES THAT SOUND, SPITSY?

WURF!

M _____

R._____

W_____

R_____

I _____

GOOD DAD

H _____

T_____

THAT'S **GOOD**, NATE! THAT'S... REALLY... UH... **GOOD!**

PAT! PAT!

A _____

R _____

TOO PERFECT

U _____

R _____

P _____

R _____

I _____

N _____

C _____

I _____

P _____

A _____

LIKES TO LECTURE

N _____

IN CHARGE

C _____

H _____

O _____

L _____

SEES EVERYTHING

CLEAN UP THIS MESS!

M _____

R _____

S. _____

E _____

VERY ARTISTIC

E _____

R _____

E _____

T _____

T _____

THE ULTIMATE MASCOT

START

Which mascot is the best?

FINISH

SWITCH IT UP!

When Nate hurts his wrist, he (gasp!) has to draw with his left hand! If you had to switch to your other hand to draw, what would your art look like? Try it!

HERE'S NATE'S LEFT-HANDED DRAWING! ⟶

ARE YOU BETTER THAN NATE?

REPLICATION STATION

Can you create cool comix characters like Nate? Find your inner artist! Draw each of these characters in the blank boxes below.

■ • �"■ ◨'■　◨◨◧◉-▽�♦-•▬▬
•▽•◆◨⊞!

▶⊞◨◈▽▬▬•!

◨　▬⊞▬◸◨◆!

DEE DEE'S DREAM ROLES

Dee Dee was born to be a star! Fill in the grid so that each of her dream roles appears only once in every row, column, and box.

W = **WENDY DARLING**

A = **ANNIE**

C = **CINDERELLA**

J = **JULIET CAPULET**

SUPER SPY

Write the following urgent messages using the top secret code you created on page 122.

N A T E   W I L L
_ ◆ ∧ _   ▭ _ _ _

S U R P A S S   A L L
||| _ _ ⬆ ◆ ||| ||| ◆ _ _

O T H E R S !
⌐ ∧ _ _ _ ||| !

A L W A Y S   A V O I D
◆ _ ▭ ◆ _ ||| ◆ _ ⌐ _ //

E G G   S A L A D !
_ ⟩ ⟩ ||| ◆ _ ◆ // !

GOOD IDEA.

W A T C H   O U T
▭ ◈ ﹀ _ _   ⌐ _ ﹀

F O R   A R T U R .
_ ⌐ _   ◈ _ ﹀ _ _ .

H E ' S   T O O
_ _ ' ⫿⫿⫿   ﹀ ⌐ ⌐

P E R F E C T !
⬆ _ _ _ _ _ ﹀ !

N E V E R   L E T
_ _ _ _ _   _ _ ﹀

R A N D Y
_ ◈ _ _ ∥ _

N E A R   Y O U !
_ _ _ ◈   _ _ ⌐ _ !

SNOW DAY

School's out and it's time to play! See if you can find all 20 of these wintry words in the word scramble on the opposite page.

SLEDDING

SKIING

TOBOGGAN

SNOWBALL

FROST

ICE-SKATING

VACATION

GLOVES

HOT CHOCOLATE

SNOWBOARDING

ICICLES

INNER TUBING

WINTER

DECEMBER

HOLIDAY

STORM

COLD

FREEZING

BOOTS

PARKA

```
D K I W I A I C C G G K W S
H C R F R E E Z I N G E I R
W O R G E G O G I I T G N E
M L L T G N N B V I S R T B
T D N I B I U S E K O A E M
N F N G D T G E G S L G R E
G N I D R A O B W O N S I C
S A E E K K Y B C B O N G E
I L N R G S T O O B O O K D
S N A O R E H N T G M W S I
I P I C I C L E S R G B I N
V A C A T I O N O A M A O I
A G L O V E S T R C E L N M
A U H G O I S L F O G L R I
```

ENEMY TERRITORY

When Nate's school, P.S. 38, is shut down temporarily, he has to attend Jefferson, their <u>ultimate</u> rival! Oh no! Solve the puzzle and see how much you know about these competing schools.

ACROSS

3. The teacher who runs Jefferson's cartooning club.

4. Who's the meanest bully at Jefferson?

7. P.S. 38's biggest bully.

9. Teddy's new snow toy is ruined by Jefferson kids. What is it called?

DOWN

1. Nate's favorite teacher runs P.S. 38's cartooning club.

2. The principal at P.S. 38.

5. The name of P.S. 38's official cartooning club.

6. Instead of a cafetorium, Jefferson kids have lunch at the _____.

8. What is Jefferson Middle School's mascot? Hint: he wears a suit of armor.

CREATE-A-CLUB

Nate is the president of the Doodlers, P.S. 38's cartooning club. If you could create your own club, what would it be?

DRAW LINES FROM LIST A TO LIST B TO MAKE SUPER-FUN CLUBS!

List A

Drama

Karaoke

Karate

Scrabble

Artistic

Math

Singing

Dance

Brainiac

Fantasy

Comedy

Sci-fi

Food-loving

List B

Masters

Queens

All-stars

Kings

Company

Sensation

Nation

Whizzes

Creation

Dynamos

Company

Connection

Spectacular

WRITE YOUR
COOL CLUB
NAMES HERE!

Supa	Stargazerz

WHAT YOU NEED IS A PLACE WHERE DRAWING CARTOONS IS WHAT YOU'RE **SUPPOSED** TO DO!

MOMENT OF GENIUS!!

HOOP IT UP!

Help Nate's team beat Jefferson.
Finish the comic and take Nate to victory!

YOUR TITLE HERE

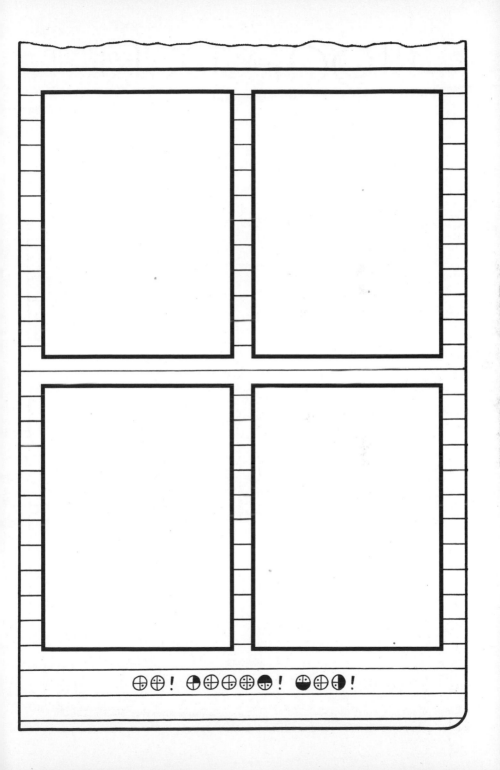

FOOD COURT GOURMET

Nate loves yummy snacks, like his ultimate choice: Cheez Doodles! Rank these food court favorites from 1 to 10. Then circle the food that surpasses all others!

SLOPPY JOE ——

NACHOS SUPREME ——

GRILLED CHEESE SANDWICH ——

SOFT-SERVE ICE CREAM ——

FRIED RICE ——

TURKEY BURGER ——

CHEESE FRIES ——

CHIPWICH ——

ONION RINGS ——

PIZZA ——

STRAWBERRY SMOOTHIE ——

CHICKEN QUESADILLA ——

CAN I HAVE A SNACK?

NAME GAME DELUXE

Can you outsmart the amazing brainiac Gina? Using the letters in Gina's name, how many other words can you make? If you find 25, you get an A++!

GINA HEMPHILL-TOMS

1.
2.
3.
4.
5. melt
6.
7.
8. pill
9.
10.
11.
12.
13.
14. most
15.

16.
17. games
18.
19.
20.
21.
22.
23.
24.
25. mule

TUNE TIME

Did you know Nate's in an über-awesome band?
Help Nate write new songs!

**FINISH THESE LYRICS—
RHYME WITH THE
UNDERLINED WORD.**

Oh Jenny, don't go <u>away</u>,

Please, baby, won't you _____?

You're the ketchup on my <u>fries</u>,

With you, there's always sunny _____.

That Artur is never <u>funny</u>,

So stick with me, my sweet _____.

Your hair is gold, like the <u>cheese</u>

On crunchy doodles. More, _____!

I'll see you at the Beach Party <u>Dance</u>,

Please, won't you give me a _____?

TO THE RESCUE

Chad has a sore butt.

Who will come to his rescue?

BEST DRAWINGS EVER!

Get your pencil! It's time for a serious drawing dare! Draw a comic using a snowman, Nolan, Nate, and . . . stewed prunes!

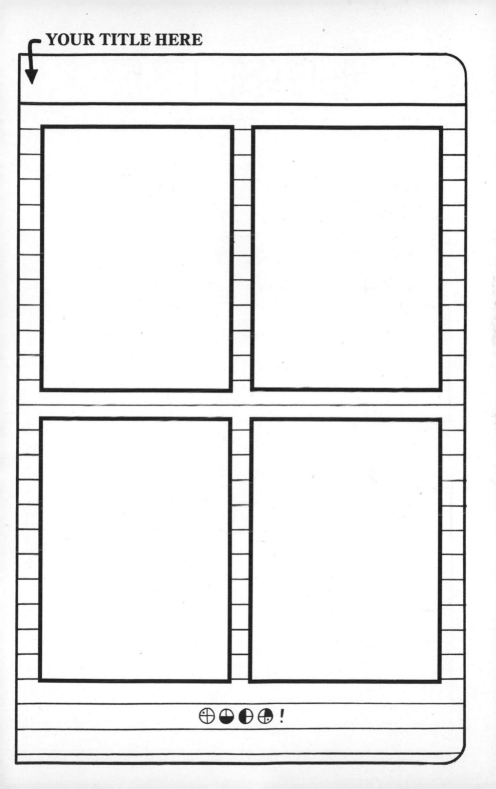

YOUR TITLE HERE

HIDE-AND-SEEK

How many items can you find in this
cool closet of old stuff? List them below!

1.	13.
2.	14.
3. trophy	15.
4.	16.
5.	17.
6.	18.
7. stuffed owl	19.
8.	20.
9.	21.
10.	22.
11.	23.
12.	24.

SCRIBBLE
BREAK!

Take a scribble-game break.

Don't forget the caption!

BRAIN BOWL

Are you a seriously BIG fan of Nate? Prove it!

DO YOU THINK THESE STATEMENTS ARE TRUE OR FALSE?

1. Nate once played T-ball for Little Ducklings Day Care.

☐ TRUE   ☐ FALSE

2. Nate's crush, Jenny, joins the Doodlers.

YOUR drawing is the bestest, Snookie Bear!

☐ TRUE   ☐ FALSE

3. Nate has a date for the Beach Party Dance.

☐ TRUE   ☐ FALSE

4. The steepest sledding hill in Nate's town is called Pinedew Peak.

☐ TRUE   ☐ FALSE

5. Dee Dee dresses up as a cavalier for the big game.

☐ TRUE   ☐ FALSE

6. Nate's all-time favorite lunch is an egg salad sandwich.
☐ TRUE   ☐ FALSE

7. Dee Dee performed Calvin Coolidge's life story as an interpretive dance.
☐ TRUE   ☐ FALSE

8. Nate gets hypnotized by Teddy's uncle Pedro.
☐ TRUE   ☐ FALSE

9. Dee Dee's middle name is Dorcas.
☐ TRUE   ☐ FALSE

10. Mr. Rosa has a dog.
☐ TRUE   ☐ FALSE

**EXTRA CREDIT!

11. Nate doesn't wear pants to the dance.
☐ TRUE   ☐ FALSE

12. Mrs. Godfrey moves to a new house.
☐ TRUE   ☐ FALSE

THE MANY FACES OF DEE DEE

Dee Dee knows drama, that's for sure! Match each face on the left with the correct emotion on the right.

CONFIDENT

TRIUMPHANT

ANNOYED

SHOCKED

MELODRAMATIC

ANGRY

EXCITED

HOOPS NIGHTMARE

Can the Jefferson cavaliers be defeated?!

SCHOOL DAZE

Imagine your dream school—what would it look like? Check pages 21–22 for Mrs. Hickson's review of the parts of speech.

MAKE A LIST OF THE COOLEST WORDS YOU CAN THINK OF:

1. Noun:

2. Plural noun:

3. Plural noun:

4. Adjective:

5. Noun:

6. Adjective:

7. Noun:

8. Verb:

9. Verb:

10. Noun: _____

11. Verb (past tense): _____

12. Adjective: _____

13. Noun: _____

14. Adjective: _____

15. Noun: _____

16. Noun: _____

17. Adjective: _____

18. Noun: _____

19. Adjective: _____

Turn the page and use your list to fill in the blanks!

I walk into _____ School,
1.

where there are _____ instead
2.

of lockers and many _____
3.

on the playground. There's also

a _____ slide that leads to a
4.

_____ , where there's a
5.

_____ machine that serves
6.

_____ . It's delicious! At recess
7.

we _____ and
8.

_____ on this
9.

huge _____ .
10.

The teachers never _____ 11. ,

and all the students get _____ 12.

_____ 13. . There

are no bullies, because

this place is so perfectly

_____ 14. . We have a _____ 15.

instead of a gym so that we can play

_____ 16. . Our mascot is the

_____ 17. _____ 18. because

we feel _____ 19. all the time!

FRUIT-TASTIC

Dee Dee wears one wild hat to the Beach Party Dance— it's covered in fruit! Solve the puzzle and uncover all the fun fruits on her head.

ACROSS

2. Rhymes with a fabulous dance called the "tango." This fruit is found in the country of Brazil.

6. One drool-worthy dessert combines this little red fruit with whipped cream and shortcake!

9. Sometimes New York City goes by the same name, the "Big _____."

10. This round fruit is the same color as its name!

DOWN

1. Juicy and sweet, this fruit's name rhymes with "beach."

3. Rhymes with "apes," this fruit comes in different colors: green, red, and purple.

4. The first syllable of the name of this fruit is also the name of a tree that rhymes with "fine."

5. Young George Washington once cut down a tree like this!

7. Monkeys love to eat these!

8. Rhymes with "yum." Purple and delicious—mmmm.

TEACHER
TWISTER

Quick! Unscramble the letters to uncover each of Nate's teachers' names... or he might stay in detention ... forever!!!

| O | H | C | A | C | | O | H | J | N |

| T | S | . | | P | M | A | L | R | E | S |

V G . N A M R L I

_____

E R G . M S O R D Y F

_____

 R R . O M S A

_____

S M . L E C K A R

_____

DISASTER DAY

Oh no!! What happened before each dire moment?
Draw it immediately!

GROSS-OUT GAME!

Nate is one messy guy—if you can actually gross HIM out, you win! Use the words below to fill in the blanks on the opposite page to create the grossest things ever!

C – C – C...
✳ KOFF! ✳

Slug	Slimy	Toe Jam
Booger	Brains	Crusty
Mold	Pickle	Liver
Egg	Possum	Soap Scum
Stinky	Ferret	Cockroach
Ear Wax	Vomit	Rat
Smelly Sock	Beetle	Rotten Banana
Bug Guts	Garbage	Dog Poop
Sour Milk	Mud	Grease

1. _____ and _____ sandwich

2. Super _____ shake

3. _____ , _____ sneakers

4. Grilled _____ and _____ kabob

5. _____ and _____ sundae

with _____ on top

6. _____ _____ hat

7. Melty _____ and _____ omelet

8. _____ and _____ T-shirt

9. A quesadilla with _____ and warm

_____ with _____ sauce

10. _____ and _____ stew

DUPLICATION NATION

Grab your pencil and get ready to draw!
How fast can you copy each character?

FUNNY BUSINESS

Nate's friend Teddy loves to crack jokes!
Use the code on page 12 to find out the punch lines.

Q: What did baby corn say to mamma corn?

A: ' ⊕
⊕⊕⊕⊕⊕⊕⊕ ?

_ _ _ _ _ _' _

_ _ _ _ _ _ _ ?

Q: What do you get when you put three ducks in a box?

A: ⊕ ⊕⊕● ⊕⊕
●⊕⊕⊕⊕⊕⊕⊕ !

_ _ _ _ _ _

_ _ _ _ _ _ _ !

Q: What do cats call mice on skateboards?

A:

_ _ _ _ _ _ _ _

_ _ _ _ _ _ _ _ !

Q: What did one firefly say to the other?

A:

_ _ _ _ _

_ _ _ _ _ _ _ !

Q: Where do fish put their money?

A:

_ _ _ _ _ _ _ _ _ _ _ .

NATE'S FAR-OUT FACTS!

Do you know all there is to know about
Nate's world? Test your Nate knowledge!

1. Who once had a glob of peanut butter stuck
to his head?

a. Coach John

b. Teddy Ortiz

c. Mr. Galvin

d. Glenn Swenson

e. Nate's dad

THANKS TO A GLOB OF PEANUT BUTTER!

2. Which girl is a member of the Doodlers?

a. Mary Ellen Popowski

b. Dee Dee

c. Ellen

d. Gina

e. Kim Cressly

...SO DO SOME RECRUITING, YOU THREE! HOP TO IT!

3. What's the name of Jefferson Middle School's principal?

a. Ms. Clarke

b. Principal Nichols

c. Mrs. Everett

d. Mrs. Williger

e. Mrs. Ortiz

...AND I AM SO HAPPY YOU'RE HERE!

4. Who designs the best posters at P.S. 38?

a. Mrs. Czerwicki

b. Mr. Rosa

c. Dee Dee

d. Gina

e. Jenny

SHE DESIGNS ALL THE POSTERS FOR THE SCHOOL PLAYS!

5. What does Nate wear to the school dance?

a. a Hawaiian shirt

b. swim trunks

c. Coach John's shorts

d. his scout uniform

e. a hula skirt and tank top

UH... RANDY TOOK MY CLOTHES.

⊕⊕⊕⊕⊕ ⊕⊕, ⊕⊕⊕⊕⊕!

ANSWER KEY

NATE-TASTIC TRIVIA (pp. 1–2)

1. True   2. True   3. False
4. True   5. False   6. True
7. False   8. True   9. False
10. False

CLOSET CRISIS! (p. 7)

DANCE DISASTERS (p. 5)

Q	S	F	K
F	K	Q	S
S	F	K	Q
K	Q	S	F

WARM FUZZIES (p. 8)

SERIOUSLY SMART (pp. 10–11)

A dragonfly has a lifespan of twenty-four hours.
Crickets hear through their knees.
The average hen will lay two hundred and twenty-seven eggs a year.

LIFE IS A DRAMA (pp. 12–13)

Poor Jenny!
Just hanging around!
Being a salesman isn't easy!
Spitsy watches TV?
What's the bird saying?

WURF!

AMAZING ARTUR (p. 17)

Code: Yes . . . amazingly annoying!

CLUB CENTRAL (p. 25)

DISGUISE MASTER (p. 33)

B	S	H	P
P	H	S	B
S	P	B	H
H	B	P	S

COMIC RELEIF (pp. 36–37)

Twelve months

Great food but no atmosphere

Because the captain was standing on the deck

DROOL-A-THON (pp. 34–35)

```
. . . . . M . . . . T . . . . . . . .
. . C U P C A K E S . A . . . S . I .
    3                          4   5
. . . . . C . . . . . C . . . P . C .
. . . . . A . C H O C O L A T E . . .
              6     7
. . . . . R . . . . . H . . . G . C .
. . H O T D O G . . . E . . . H . R .
  8
. . . . . N . . C . . E . . . E . E .
              9
. . . . . I . H . . . Z . . . T . A .
. . S T E A K · E . . D . . . T . M .
  10
. . . . . N . R . . . O . . . I . . .
. P . . S O D A . R . O . . . . . . .
 11    12
. O . . . C . . Y . D . . . . . . . .
. P . . . H . . P . L . . . . . . . .
. C H I C K E N F I N G E R S . . . .
 13
. O . . . E . . E . S . . . . . . . .
. R . . . S . . . . . . . . . . . . .
. N . C H E E S E . . . . . . . . . .
    14
```

ON THE SPOT (pp. 39–40)
1. (c.) Teddy
2. (c.) Mrs. Czerwicki
3. (c.) Tap Dancing
4. (a.) Jenny
5. (d.) Gina

ARCHRIVALS (p. 41)

LAP OF LUXURY (pp. 42–43)
Code: Sweet!
Totally awesome!

BACK TO NATURE (p. 54)
Sweet
A giant sequoia tree

TOGETHERVILLE (p. 63)
1. C 4. B
2. D 5. A
3. E

AWESOME ADD-ONS (p. 65)

R	E	M	D	H	S	B	T	L
B	T	S	E	L	R	H	D	M
H	D	L	B	M	T	E	S	R
E	S	H	R	T	B	M	L	D
L	M	D	H	S	E	R	B	T
T	B	R	M	D	L	S	H	E
S	R	B	L	E	D	T	M	H
D	H	E	T	B	M	L	R	S
M	L	T	S	R	H	D	E	B

SCHOOL SPIRIT (pp. 46–47)
Cavalier
Tigers
Lions
Eagles
Bears
Bulls
Rams

MYTH MADNESS (p. 49)

A	P	H	C	M	Z
Z	C	M	A	H	P
C	M	A	Z	P	H
P	H	Z	M	A	C
M	Z	P	H	C	A
H	A	C	P	Z	M

GROWN-UP GOSSIP (pp. 60–61)
He smells!
Watch out!
Godzilla.
Gross!

MIX-AND-MATCH MAYHEM (p. 56)
1. D
2. C
3. E
4. A
5. B

CALLING ALL CARTOONISTS (p. 62)

YARD SALE SCRAMBLE (p. 71)

SURF'S UP! (p. 81)

MOVE OVER, DR. DOLITTLE (pp. 74–75)

Camels have three eyelids.

Horses cannot vomit.

Goats' eyes have rectangular pupils.

MODEL TIMBER SCOUT (p. 79)

PRINCIPAL'S POP QUIZ! (pp. 82–83)

1. (c.) Dee Dee
2. (b.) Randy
3. (c.) Mold
4. (d.) Beach Party
5. (b.) Green bean incident

ELIMINATION STATION (p. 85)

Nate's fleeceball game is not: A yawn-a-thon

Nate's sister, Ellen, is not: Shy

Detention is not: Dazzling

The cafetorium is not: Fancy

Doodlers are not: Scary

Nate's rival, Artur, is not: Wild

BE TRUE TO YOUR SCHOOL (p. 91)

1. P.S. 38
2. Jefferson
3. P.S. 38
4. P.S. 38
5. Jefferson

ART ATTACK (pp. 102–103)

BIG NATE TRIVIA BONANZA (pp. 100–101)

Artur wins the second-place prize. 3

Nate spits up green beans all over the cafetorium. 1

Nate's locker explodes all over Randy. 2

Mrs. Godfrey sends Nate to detention. 1

Nate and Gina become partners! 2

Chad has to use a donut when sitting down. 4

Nate Gets an A! (How did that happen?) 2 or 5

WHAT HAPPENS NEXT?
(pp. 104–105)
That hurt!
Will Nate get revenge?
Oh, the drama!
That bully!

DRAMA QUEEN (p. 107)

FRUITOPIA (p. 111)

B	G	P	O
O	P	G	B
P	B	O	G
G	O	B	P

CHILL OUT! (pp. 114–115)
Sledding
Snow boarding
Snowball fight
Skiing
Building a snowman
Ice-skating
Drinking cocoa

JOKING AROUND (pp. 116–117)
A potato!
Don't look! I'm changing!
Meet me at the corner!
A comb!
It did not want to be a hot dog!

REWIND (p. 129)
Code: Watch out, Nate!

CONSTRUCTION JUNCTION (p. 125)

U	A	R	H	T	F	I	L	K	R	O	F	E	R	H
A	P	K	R	H	O	E	T	D	E	W	E	B	E	L
L	N	C	E	E	A	O	R	L	R	A	X	A	O	N
C	E	U	D	N	D	F	L	E	E	T	C	R	H	L
P	E	R	A	L	O	I	N	B	R	H	A	E	T	R
R	A	T	O	H	R	C	L	V	E	R	V	D	T	I
B	D	P	L	D	H	E	C	R	N	L	A	D	E	R
U	L	M	E	A	S	U	R	I	N	G	T	A	P	E
L	K	U	O	I	R	Y	H	H	F	H	O	L	W	L
L	S	D	H	E	P	W	A	C	A	F	R	L	I	C
D	V	C	K	I	C	I	N	R	C	F	A	D	U	E
O	A	S	C	R	E	W	D	R	I	V	E	R	C	A
Z	A	K	A	K	N	H	S	H	O	V	E	L	T	E
E	E	N	B	H	A	C	A	T	E	D	A	I	E	C
R	E	S	I	T	F	I	W	B	S	O	D	I	L	K

CLUB BONANZA (p. 137)

K	W	B	S	D	P
P	S	D	W	B	K
W	D	P	B	K	S
S	B	K	P	W	D
D	P	W	K	S	B
B	K	S	D	P	W

POSTER PASSION
(p. 139)
Code: Totally cool!

ROCK ON! (pp. 130–131)

	¹S	P	O	T	L	I	²G	H	T
	I						U		
	N		³M	U	S	I	C		
	G						T		
	E				⁴F	A	N	⁵S	
⁶D	R	U	M	⁷S			R		O
				T					L
		⁸B	A	N	D				O
				G					
		⁹B	E	A	T				

SUPER NATE, SUPER FAST
(pp. 140–141)
1. (b.) Cosmic Cat
2. (e.) snow sculpture contest
3. (d.) dog
4. (b.) food court
5. (b.) Supa-Sno Tube

SUPER SNOW SCULPTOR
(pp. 158–159)
Code: Nice top hat!
Dee Dee's dramatic snowman!
So cool!

ALL SHOOK UP!
(pp. 148–149)
Nolan
Mr. Staples
Teddy
Jenny
Ellen
Kim Cressly
Francis
Coach John
Artur

SPORTS SNAPSHOT
(pp.152–153)
Code: Nate loves to win!
How old were you?

INSIDER INFO
(pp. 160–161)
1. (c.) yogurt
2. (b.) Achilles
3. (d.) a cavalier
4. (c.) Trying to catch Chad's donut
Code: Wow, you are a genius!

COOLEST-CLUB CHALLENGE (p. 157)

```
R H O I N O I T A S N E S G N I G N I S
E D E R E E S I I O S A E T G S S T N Y
F S B F B K N R P A E I N S N P R E N S
N R C A Y D O A R I D R E A M T E A M E
W E R C E C I V R E S Y T I N U M M O C
N N A T A E C S R T G C V G Q O Y F C N
S O F A R O S N H M Y R A E R M H E R A
C O T S B A I P I C M M C I T V R A U I
S R C T O S F G P A N N M E N S D A C L
I C L I O A I S C U A U A Y A I N C T L
C E U C K A C E R D S I B R I M A E I A
G K B F C P S F P I T N F K B R P R R S
T O A E O R T O C E I K T E O E A R B T
S A R W M T M B E C I H G U O R R Y S I
C R F O M P A T H E S P I A N S B E S I
A A K S I S R E M A G T A E R G O N L T
A K I H T S K A T E R B R I G A D E N R
A A E E T O T I N V O S O F P U C N I A
I A R O E A S R R F U N P A T R O L R K
T S E T E L H T A M P A M E S A E C E R
```

Code: What's your passion?

THE ULTIMATE MASCOT
(p. 164)

REPLICATION STATION (p. 167)
Code: Nate's know-it-all sister!
Godzilla!
A bobcat!

DEE DEE'S DREAM ROLES (p. 169)

J	C	A	W
W	A	J	C
C	J	W	A
A	W	C	J

SNOW DAY (p. 173)

```
D K I W I A I C C G G K W S
H C R F R E E Z I N G E I R
W O R G E G O G I I T G N E
M L L T G N N B V I S R T B
T D N I B I U S E K O A E M
N F N G D T G E G S L G R E
G N I D R A O B W O N S I C
S A E S K K Y B C B O N G E
I L N R G S T O X B O O K D
S N A O R E H N T G M W S I
I P I C I C L E S R G B I N
V A C A T I O N O A M A O I
A G L O V E S T R C E L N M
A U H G O I S L F O G L R I
```

ENEMY TERRITORY (pp. 174–175)

		¹M				²P						
³M	R	S	E	V	E	R	E	T	T			
		R				I						
⁴N	O	L	A	N		N						
		S				C						
		A				I						
				⁵D		P						
	⁶F			O		A			⁸C			
	O			O		L		⁷R	A	N	D	Y
	O			D		N			V			
	D			L		I			A			
	C			E		C			L			
	O			R		H			I			
⁹S	U	P	A	S	N	O	T	U	B	E		
	R					L			R			
	T					S						

BEST DRAWINGS EVER (p. 185)
Code: Yuck!

BRAIN BOWL (pp. 188–189)
1. True   2. False   3. True
4. False   5. False   6. False
7. True   8. True   9. True
10. True   11. True   12. True

FRUIT-TASTIC (pp. 196–197)

	¹P									
	E									
²M	A	N	³G	O						
	C		R		⁴P			⁵C		
	H		A		I			H		
			P		N			F		
			E		E			R		
		⁶S	T	R	A	W	⁷B	E	R	R	Y
			P		A		Y			
			P		N		⁸P			
			L		⁹A	P	P	L	E	
	¹⁰O	R	A	N	G	E		U		
					A			M		
					S					

FUNNY BUSINESS (pp. 206–207)
Where's popcorn?
A box of quackers!
Meals on wheels!
Got to glow now!
In riverbanks.

HOOP IT UP! (p. 179)
Code: Go! Fight! Win!

TO THE RESCUE (p. 183)

HOOPS NIGHTMARE (p. 191)

TEACHER TWISTER (pp. 198–199)
Coach John
Mr. Staples
Mr. Galvin
Mrs. Godfrey
Mr. Rosa
Ms. Clarke

NATE'S FAR-OUT FACTS! (pp. 208–209)
1. (d.) Glenn Swenson
2. (b.) Dee Dee
3. (d.) Mrs. Williger
4. (c.) Dee Dee
5. (e.) a hula skirt and tank top
Code: Party on, dude!

"ZONED" OUT!

You know what? Only a week ago, my life totally stunk.

ExCUSE me, but the CORRECT word would be "stank."

Okay, then — it STANK. Gina was being her usual know-it-all self...

Artur and Jenny were going over-board with the PDOs*...

nuzzle nuzzle

Ugh.

(*Public Displays of Obnoxiousness)

And worst of all: last week, REPORT CARDS got mailed home.

Ellen, I can't BELIEVE these GRADES!

Nate, I can't BELIEVE these grades.

Then — I'm not sure how, but it had something to do with Chad — my luck changed. Suddenly, I'm **IN THE ZONE!**

Congratulations, Nate! You're on the **HONOR ROLL!**

Nate, you made the league **ALL-STAR TEAM!**

Hiiiiii, Nate!

SHOVE!

I've **NEVER** had a hot streak like this before. The question is: **HOW LONG WILL IT LAST??**

Not very long!

Maybe good luck isn't everything it's cracked up to be!

Read **BIG NATE IN THE ZONE!**

"Big Nate is funny, big time."
—Jeff Kinney, author of Diary of a Wimpy Kid

BIG NATE
IN THE ZONE

Lincoln Peirce

Lincoln Peirce

(pronounced "purse") is a cartoonist/writer and *New York Times* bestselling author of the hilarious Big Nate book series (www.bignatebooks.com), now published in twenty-five countries worldwide and available as ebooks and audiobooks and as an app, Big Nate: Comix by U! He is also the creator of the comic strip *Big Nate*. It appears in over three hundred U.S. newspapers and online daily at www.gocomics.com/bignate. Lincoln's boyhood idol was Charles Schulz of *Peanuts* fame, but his main inspiration for Big Nate has always been his own experience as a sixth grader. Just like Nate, Lincoln loves comics, ice hockey, and Cheez Doodles (and dislikes cats, figure skating, and egg salad). His Big Nate books have been featured on *Good Morning America* and in the *Boston Globe*, the *Los Angeles Times*, *USA Today*, and the *Washington Post*. He has also written for Cartoon Network and Nickelodeon. Lincoln lives with his wife and two children in Portland, Maine.

For exclusive information
on your favorite authors and artists,
visit www.authortracker.com.